OLD ROCK

(is not boring)

Deb Pilutti

putnam

G. P. PUTNAM'S SONS

For Jack,

who's never boring.

Special thanks to Larry Lemke, Ph.D.,

and Lacey Knowles, Ph.D.,

for sharing their knowledge

of the natural world with me.

G. P. PUTNAM'S SONS
an imprint of Penguin Random House LLC, New York

Copyright © 2020 by Deb Pilutti
Penguin supports copyright. Copyright fuels creativity, encourages diverse voices,
promotes free speech, and creates a vibrant culture. Thank you for buying an authorized edition of
this book and for complying with copyright laws by not reproducing, scanning, or distributing any part of it in any
form without permission. You are supporting writers and allowing Penguin to continue to publish books for every reader.

G. P. Putnam's Sons is a registered trademark of Penguin Random House LLC.

Visit us online at penguinrandomhouse.com

Library of Congress Cataloging-in-Publication Data
Names: Pilutti, Deb, author, illustrator.
Title: Old Rock (is not boring) / Deb Pilutti.
Description: New York, NY : G. P. Putnam's Sons, [2020]
Summary: Tall Pine, Spotted Beetle, and Hummingbird are certain that
being a rock is boring until Old Rock shares what he has seen and done since
he first flew out of a volcano.
Identifiers: LCCN 2018008836 (print) | LCCN 2018015908 (ebook) |
ISBN 9780525518198 (ebook) | ISBN 9780525518181 (hardcover)
Subjects: | CYAC: Rocks—Fiction.
Classification: LCC PZ7.P6318 (ebook) | LCC PZ7.P6318 Old 2020 (print) | DDC [E]—dc23
LC record available at https://lccn.loc.gov/2018008836

Manufactured in China by RR Donnelley Asia Printing Solutions Ltd.
ISBN 9780525518181
10 9 8 7 6 5 4 3 2

Design by Semadar Megged and Dave Kopka
Text set in Neutraface Text
The illustrations in this book were done with casein on watercolor paper and a bit of digital painting.

OLD ROCK had been sitting
in the same spot,
at the edge of a clearing
in the middle of a pine forest,
for as long as anyone could remember.

And even before that.

"Being a rock seems awfully boring," said Tall Pine.

"You sit in the same spot, day after day,"
said Spotted Beetle.

"It's a very nice spot," said Old Rock.

"Don't you want to go anywhere?"
asked Hummingbird.

"I've flown all over the world and
sipped the nectar of exotic flowers.
I would surely be bored if I could not fly."

"I flew once," said Old Rock.

"Gosh!"
said Tall Pine.

"How?"
asked Spotted Beetle.

"Rocks don't fly,"
said Hummingbird.

Old Rock told them about the time
in the beginning, when darkness
was all around . . .

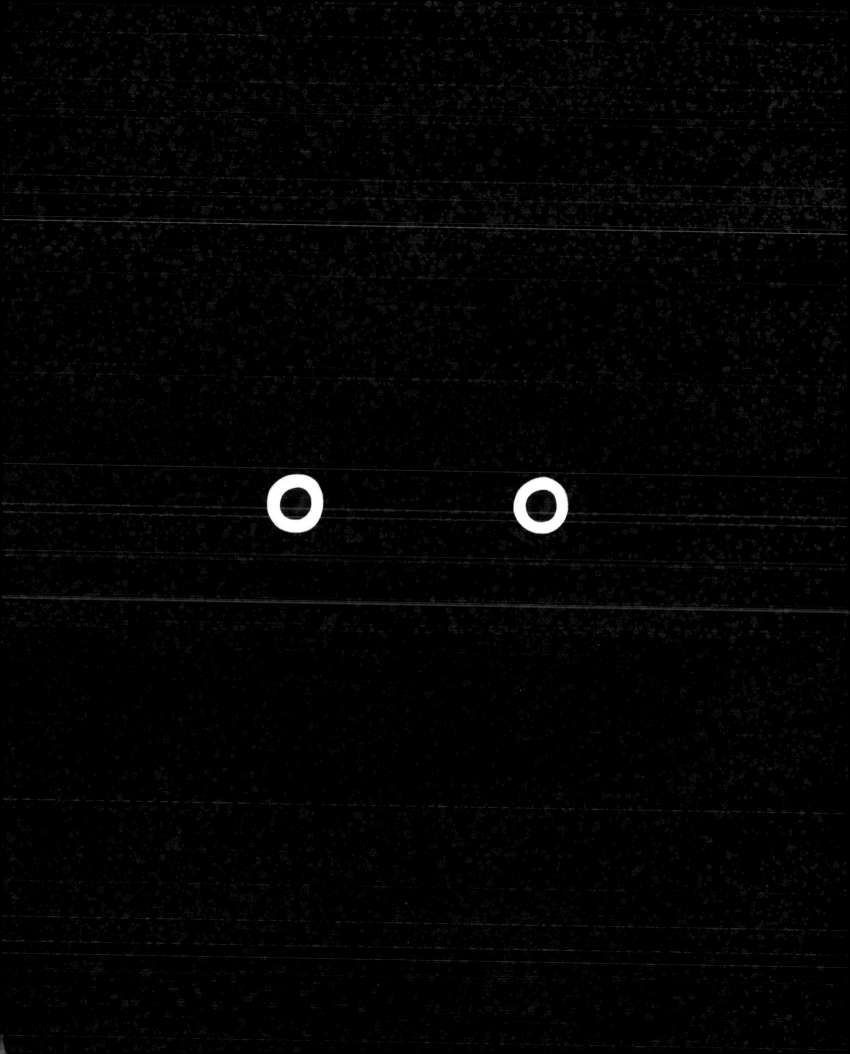

"And then I erupted out of a volcano
and soared through a fiery sky
into the bright light of a new world."

"So it was just the one time,"
said Hummingbird.

"And now you're sitting here,"
said Tall Pine.

"Being bored," said Spotted Beetle.

"I'm not bored," said Old Rock.

"Don't you want to see more?"
asked Spotted Beetle.

"If I climb to the tip-top branch of Tall Pine,
I might see a deer mouse nibbling seeds
in a nearby tree,

or watch ships sailing
across the big lake."

Old Rock said, "I've seen a lot."

Old Rock told them about the time
a group of friendly dinosaurs lumbered by,
munching every leaf in sight.

Time passed,
  things changed,

and the world chilled.

Which wasn't too bad, because
Old Rock took a ride in a glacier
and toured the land.

"Once the glacier melted, it left me perched
at the top of a ridge, and
I could see the place
where the sky touches the earth."

"My, you have seen a lot,"
said Spotted Beetle.

"How unusual,"
said Hummingbird.

"Yes, but that was ages ago,"
said Tall Pine.

"Aren't you bored now?
Don't you want to move?
My limbs flutter gently in a breeze
and dance wildly when the wind blows."

"I've never danced, but I'm pretty good
at doing somersaults," said Old Rock.

Old Rock revealed that after teetering on the ridge
for a while, the ground rumbled . . .

"And I tumbled and stumbled

down,

down,

down into a valley."

Grasses grew, mastodons roamed,
and lakes formed.

"I never knew a rock had moves like that!"
said Tall Pine.

"I wish I could have seen those things,"
said Spotted Beetle.

"What happened next?"
asked Hummingbird.

"A pine forest sprouted up around me.
One day, a strong breeze shook a pinecone loose.
From the pinecone, a seed fell
onto the forest floor.

I watched that seedling grow to be the tall pine
who dances in the wind
and keeps me company.

Sometimes, a spotted beetle wanders
along to report
all that he sees.

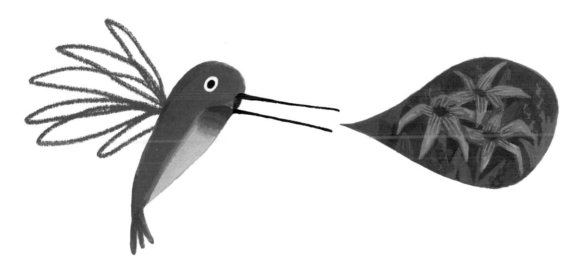

And every so often, the loveliest hummingbird
stops to rest after a long flight,
and she describes the amazing places
she's visited."

"It's a very nice spot," said Old Rock.

"Yes, it is," agreed Tall Pine.

"Very nice," said Spotted Beetle.

"Not boring at all," said Hummingbird.

1.8 BILLION YEARS AGO

Old Rock forms deep under the earth's crust.

Metamorphic rocks are created with extreme heat and pressure. It can take millions of years for a metamorphic rock to form.

300 MILLION YEARS AGO

A volcano erupts and Old Rock is blasted into the sky.

During a pyroclastic eruption, gases, ash, rocks and lava blobs can be ejected.

150 MILLION YEARS AGO

Old Rock chats with a friendly dinosaur.

Gigantic sauropods, like the brachiosaur, appeared during the Jurassic Period.

66 MILLION YEARS AGO

Old Rock meets a hungry T. rex.

Tyrannosaurus rex lived during the Cretaceous Period, which ended 65.5 million years ago.

2.6 MILLION YEARS AGO

Old Rock begins a journey in a glacier.

Glaciers covered much of the earth's surface during the Pleistocene Epoch.

16,000 YEARS AGO

The glacier retreats and leaves Old Rock perched on a ledge.

There have been several cooling periods in earth's history.

11,000 YEARS AGO

A mastodon stops to rest.

Mastodons roamed North America for almost 24 million years until their extinction 10,000 years ago.

PRESENT DAY

Old Rock, Tall Pine, Spotted Beetle, and Hummingbird sit in a very nice spot at the edge of a clearing in the middle of a forest.

They are not bored.